A Little Rebel Becomes A Saint

Grace & Truth Books

Sand Springs, Oklahoma

ISBN # 1-58339-056-1

Originally published in the 1800's by the American Tract
    Society
Printed by Triangle Press, 1998
Current printing, Grace & Truth Books, 2004

Cover art by Caffy Whitney
Cover design by Ben Gundersen

Grace & Truth Books
3406 Summit Boulevard
Sand Springs, Oklahoma 74063
Phone: 918 245 1500

www.graceandtruthbooks.com

Table of Contents

Charles was old enough to play outside by himself.

Chapter 1

CHARLES AND HIS PUPPY

There was a time when the forests were thick with pines, and the wildlife danced through the thickets. The rivers flowed clear, and a marvelous sky covered the land. People awoke with the chirping of the sparrow and were lulled to sleep at night by the moan of the owl.

From these forests sprang much joy, but also much fear. Late in the night, wolves howled and panthers screamed. The mark of the tomahawk scarred the maple trees. On the outskirts of each village lay the graves of the victims of the savage battles fought against both man and beast. Into this world of both joy and fear, Charles was born.

Charles came from a godly family, but tragedy tore them apart early in his life. While Charles was still a babe, his father died rather suddenly of diphtheria. Without the resources to support her child alone, his mother had to give the toddler up for adoption.

Before his father died, he prayed for Charles daily. His mother constantly asked the Lord to watch over her child. Even after she was separated from her son, she still asked for God's protection and blessing over him. Each prayer of faith they offered up to God for Charles, heaven heard. His father may have left the earth, and his mother may have not been with him, but their prayers were written in God's Book of Remembrance.

Charles' mother provided no inheritance for him, but because of her prayers, Providence looked over him. A wealthy gentleman and his wife adopted the young boy. They had no children of their own, so they loved him as they would their own flesh and blood.

Charles' adopted mother, Mrs. Raymond, was a very godly lady. She was a gentle, but unbending woman. She kept God's laws and required Charles to do so too. Mr. Raymond, on the other hand, was a very wicked man. He used God's name in vain and lived for the things of the flesh.

In the early years of Charles' childhood, Mrs. Raymond began teaching him the ways of God. She strove to raise him into a worthy, God-fearing adult. One of the first lessons that she taught him was the importance of obedience.

At the age of three, Charles was running, jumping, and playing. He had a huge yard to play in, because the Raymonds owned a large farm. Seemingly endless rows of crops surrounded the yard. Since little Charles could be lost in the tall wheat so easily, Mrs. Raymond always sat outside and watched him play.

One day, however, Mrs. Raymond decided that Charles was old enough to play outside by himself. She said, "Charles, you can play outdoors by yourself, but you must abide by one rule. You cannot go outside of the fence surrounding the yard."

Mr. Raymond walked in at that moment with a squirmy, little bundle in his arms. He said, "I've got a present for you, Charles. One of the field hands gave it to me." With that, he handed Charles a playful, black puppy.

Charles was delighted. Finally, he had someone to play with. "What shall I name him, Father?"

"You can name him whatever you like, son," answered Mr. Raymond.

"How about Bobby. That's what I'll call you. You are my little, black Bobby. Come on, let's go play." Charles rushed outside to play with his newfound friend.

Charles and Bobby jumped and played within the yard for half an hour. The little puppy, however, became bored with the small area and he started walking along the fence looking out. Where the fence met the house, there was a small opening. Bobby found it and squirmed through. Charles hesitated, and then decided that he couldn't let his puppy wander off alone. Charles squeezed through the hole right after him.

Charles followed Bobby past the chicken coop and around the barn. Then they ran and played past the corral. Charles had never been this far away from home, and it was exciting. They soon came upon the long, flowing wheat fields. Little Charles

Charles squeezed through the hole right after him.

followed the puppy across the rows. They had a wonderful time exploring through the tall wheat, discovering gophers and field mice. As long as the child followed, Bobby kept running farther and farther away from home.

Weary from traveling for what seemed like hours, Charles sat down in the middle of the field to rest. The midday sun was beating down, and he was getting hungry and thirsty. "It will be time for lunch soon," thought Charles. "We should probably get home before Mother sees that we are gone."

Charles stood up, wiped his forehead, and looked around. "Which way is home?" he began to wonder. They had been running and playing so long in the tall wheat that Charles had lost track of where he was. Charles wasn't as tall as the wheat, so all he could see were the mazes of rows surrounding him and stretching on for what seemed like miles. The little boy began to cry.

"Oh, Bobby, how do we get home? If we don't get home soon, the Indians will get us. I've heard Daddy talking about the Indians. They do horrible things to little boys. We must get home or the Indians will take us. Oh, Bobby, we have to get home. How do we get home!"

As it happened, the same field hand that had given Mr. Raymond the puppy was working in that field. He heard the little boy crying and looked in that direction. All he could see was the back of the black puppy as he jumped up and down. Realizing

The terrified little boy soon felt two
strong arms pull him up out of the wheat.

what must have happened, the field hand ran across the field to Charles.

When Charles heard the man coming for him through the field, he thought that the Indians had him for sure. He cried even louder. "Please don't take me. I want to go home. Just tell me how to get home."

The terrified little boy soon felt two strong arms pull him up out of the wheat. With eyes filled with terror, Charles looked up, and there was Joe.

He cried, "Oh, Joe, you saved me. The Indians were going to come and get me. Bobby and I were just playing, and before I knew it, we were way out here in the wheat. I didn't mean to get lost. Then I heard the Indians. ...."

"It's okay now, Charles. I'm taking you home. A little boy like you shouldn't be way out here in the fields. Does your mother know where you are at?"

Then Charles remembered the rule. "Mother told me not to go outside of the fence," he thought. "I should have obeyed her."

Joe brought the naughty little boy back to Mrs. Raymond, who had been running all around the barnyard frantically looking for him.

"Charles, where have you been?" asked Mrs. Raymond.

"I found him out in the wheat field behind the barn," replied the farmhand, Joe.

Mrs. Raymond took the sniffling child from the man's hands and said, "Thank you for bringing him home. I'm sorry for the trouble."

"That's okay, Mrs. Raymond. Good afternoon," Joe said as he turned around and headed back out to the field.

The kind lady brought Charles into the house and sat down in the rocking chair to talk to him. As they rocked, she gently corrected him for disobeying her. She explained to him that disobedience was what made God send Adam and Eve out of that beautiful Garden of Eden.

Mrs. Raymond explained to Charles that great kingdoms were overthrown because of disobedience. She explained that the wisest king that ever lived, besides our Lord Jesus Christ, was punished for his disobedience.

Then she also explained to Charles that God made a very rich promise for children who honour and obey their parents. She read to him from Ephesians 6:2-3, "Honour thy father and mother; which is the first commandment with promise; That it may be well with thee, and thou mayest live long on the earth."

∽⊃✕⊂∼

Every morning, Charles and Miss Owens
made the journey to Bradburry for school.

Chapter 2

CHARLES GOES TO SCHOOL

Mrs. Raymond did her best to guide Charles through his early childhood, and it soon came time to send him to school. Soon, another adult entered his life to help teach him the right way to live.

The schoolteacher, for the town of Bradburry, rented a room in the Raymonds' home. Charles had heard so much from her about school and all of the children. Every night, Miss Owens told stories around the dinner table about what had happened in her classroom that day. Charles loved to hear her tales, and he longed for the day when he would be old enough to go too.

Miss Owens came from a wealthy family on the East coast. She left for the West to escape the evil temptations in the city. Miss Owens was a godly woman. Her godly principles and sound morals were often passed on to the children she taught. She was very civilized and kind at all times. She could be firm, however, when it became necessary.

Every morning, Charles and Miss Owens made the journey to Bradburry for school. The Raymonds' farm was a little over a mile outside of the town. Miss Owens used this time to teach

Charles godly principles. She especially warned Charles to avoid sin and to keep away from bad company. Sometimes she told him stories about Abraham, David, Joseph, and other great men in the Bible. Other times she related a part from the life of Jesus Christ.

The Bible and a spelling primer were the only books in Miss Owens' school. At that time, they were the only books that boys, who would grow into farmers and laborers, would need. Charles learned to read from the Bible almost every day. The impression that Miss Owens made on Charles' mind never left him.

There was one early morning walk with Miss Owens that would always stand apart in Charles' memory. Miss Owens gave him some advice that would help guide him through many of the troubles of life.

"Charles," she said, "You can compare your life with a journey over the sea. You have set out upon this journey at a very young age, and, of course, you will have little stability while sailing across this ocean of life. There will be surging waves and hazardous rocks along the way. You will certainly shipwreck if you don't take a certain treasure along. That treasure is the Bible. The Lord has given you this Book expressly for the voyage of life. Take it with you wherever you go."

Later that same year, Charles' mother taught him how to pray. Charles had seen both her and Miss Owens pray many times, and he wanted to learn how also. Mrs. Raymond decided that the best way to teach Charles how to pray was by example. Thus, every night before bedtime, Charles and his mother prayed together.

Charles learned that he should pray often for God's grace to be honest and honorable. Many times during the day, Charles called to mind the prayers he heard them offer to God for him. Whenever he was about to sin, these prayers always rang in his ears. Charles never forgot those prayers with his mother, or the warnings from Miss Owens.

*He took his coat out of the opening of the
hole and poured the pail of water down into it.*

Chapter 3

DROWNING THE SQUIRREL

When Charles was seven, Miss Owens taught him something that influenced the rest of his life. It happened on one of their morning walks to school.

In the last year, Charles had begun to play with a troublesome group of boys at school. At first, Charles didn't like the way the boys treated others, but the more time he spent with them, the less their evil ways bothered him.

The first time that Charles saw them kill a small animal, he was horrified. After watching their enjoyment, however, he started to change his mind. Within a few weeks, Charles was joining them in their bad games.

One morning on the way to school, Charles saw a squirrel dash into its hole by the roadside. He ran ahead of Miss Owens to find where it had gone. When Charles found the hole, he plugged it with his coat, so the little animal couldn't escape.

Charles looked around and saw the stream that the road followed. He had an idea. As quickly as he could, Charles emptied all the food from his lunch pail and ran to the stream. He filled his pail up with water and carefully carried it back to the hole.

He took his coat out of the opening of the hole and poured the pail of water down into it. Then he waited silently. Charles soon heard the squirrel coming up, struggling for life.

He whispered, "Oh, I've got you now."

About this time, Miss Owens caught up with Charles. In shock she screeched, "What are you doing, Charles?"

Thrilled, the little boy answered, "I am drowning a squirrel. Can't you hear him struggling for air right now? I will soon have him."

"Charles," Miss Owens began, "my dear boy, I am sorry to see that you have become so cruel. What harm has that little innocent squirrel done to you? How would you feel if a very big man came along and did that to you? What if you were down in that hole, and he was pouring water on you? Would you not think his behavior was cruel and wicked? Life is as sweet to that little innocent creature as it is to you. God made the squirrel to be happy. Why do you try to kill it?"

"Many years ago," the kind teacher continued, "an elderly man caught my older brother, Paul, doing the same thing you are now doing. He said the same thing to my brother that I have said to you. It affected Paul so much that he never killed another innocent creature again. I hope you will do the same."

Charles sat in shock. He hadn't even realized what he was doing. Suddenly, he felt compelled to make it right. Charles pulled the squirrel from the hole and let him go.

The young boy never forgot the lesson that Miss Owens taught him that day. Whenever an animal came his way, Charles thought of her reproof. He always respected her for it.

As they finished the journey to school, Miss Owens talked to Charles about the reason why he had been doing the horrible act to begin with. She said, "I suspect that those bad boys you have been playing with at school taught you how to hurt the poor animal."

"That is right, Miss Owens," replied Charles in a low tone.

"Charles, teaching you this horrible deed is not the only way those evil boys have hurt you. They have also hurt you in another way. When people see you in the company of wicked children, you bear the disgrace that follows their deeds. Godly people lose confidence in you."

"What do you mean, Ma'am?" asked Charles.

"You have friends, Charles, that do not keep the Sabbath day. They break it with their idle playing. They take the Lord's name in vain; they tell lies; and perhaps, they even steal. Aren't they despised by all that see them? Most godly parents don't let their children near them. Charles, don't become despised by godly people. If they despise you, they will never let their children be your friends. You will lose your chance to be around God's people."

Miss Owens continued, "Charles, choose your friends with great care. There is an old proverb, which says, 'Show me your company and I will tell you your character.' It is very true."

Charles fell silent for the rest of the journey to school. He thought about what Miss Owens said and knew she was right. He had been playing with boys who were hurting him. They were teaching him evil deeds, and they were ruining the confidence of the town's godly people in him. By the time they reached school, Charles had decided that he couldn't play with those boys anymore.

Miss Owens faithfully taught Charles these truths through the early years of his life. Like good seed, they retained their vitality. After many years of being crusted over with sin, by divine culture, these seeds yielded fruit. The dews of the Spirit, accompanied by the ploughshare of affliction, softened and prepared the soil of Charles' heart.

Chapter 4

THE FORBIDDEN SWIM

Bradburry was a very small town. Since the people could only afford to pay one schoolteacher, Miss Owens taught a wide range of students. Boys and girls of all ages crowded into the one-room schoolhouse. The oldest were the twelve-year-old boys, because the thirteen year olds had to stay home to work on their farms.

When Charles was nine, Miss Owens had five twelve-year olds in her class. The leader of the little group was Duke. At times, Duke liked to think that he was in charge of the class instead of the teacher. Miss Owens constantly disciplined Duke, but nothing seemed to help. Finally, in the spring of the school year, she got tired of his continual disobedience. Miss Owens told Duke that the next time he disobeyed she would expel him from school for good.

One day during lunch, Charles was sitting outside on a stump with his friends eating from his lunch pail. Duke and the other four older boys walked across the schoolyard to him.

"I heard that you know how to swim," Duke said to Charles.

Duke thought for a bit, then motioned all the boys to lean in really close. They listened intently to his idea.

Charles answered, "Yes, I do. One of my father's farm hands taught me."

"We want you to teach us how," Duke demanded.

Charles pondered the idea. This would be a great way for him to become a part of the older boys' group.

"Okay, I'll show you, but I can't do it after school. Father is expecting me to come home right away to help plant."

"We have to plant too," Duke answered, "but I think I know when we can go." The mischievous boy's eyes began to sparkle. A plan was forming in his mind. Duke thought for a bit, then motioned all the boys to lean in really close. They listened intently to his idea.

One by one, the boys went into the school house to tell Miss Owens that they were needed at home. They told her that their fathers needed help getting the crop planted on time. They all walked off in their separate directions until they were out of Miss Owens' sight. Then they turned around and headed for the water hole about a half mile behind the school.

Randy arrived first, and Duke quickly joined him. Then the Olson twins, James and John, came rushing through the trees. They were still laughing about the good trick they had played on Miss Owens. Ken was the last of their group to make it. They all sat down to wait for Charles.

When Charles was half way there, he stopped to think about what he was doing. He was starting to feel guilty about deceiving Miss Owens. A year ago, she had moved into town, but they were still close friends.

Then Charles remembered that all the boys were waiting for him. Visions of him becoming the new leader of the older group swam in his head. Charles just knew that everybody in the whole school would envy him.

"After all," Charles thought, "I told the boys I would meet them at the pond. If I don't go, then I will have told two lies. That certainly must be worse than just one." With that excuse, Charles ran toward the water hole.

When he arrived, he found the older boys waiting impatiently.

"Ready?" asked Charles.

"Let's go," Duke answered.

They all quickly took off their shirts and their shoes. Then one at a time they began wading into the cool water. Charles went first to make sure there weren't any deep spots.

"First," Charles said, "You have to learn to float. It's real easy. All you do is lie down in the water and let all your body go limp." Charles showed them what he was talking about. Then he stood back up and said, "Now, you guys do it."

All the boys did what Charles said, and they found that it was pretty easy. Within fifteen minutes, they were all floating around the shallow area of the pond.

"Okay, now the next step is a little bit harder …"

Charles was interrupted by a loud splashing sound behind him. He turned around and saw Duke. Without knowing it, the older boy had floated out into the deep water.

"Help! Save me!" he screamed as he disappeared under the water.

Charles dove under the surface to look for Duke. He couldn't find him, so he came back up for air and tried again. The second time, Charles saw Duke sinking to the bottom. Charles swam down to the limp boy and began dragging him to the surface. When they got Duke on shore, he still wasn't moving.

"Go get Miss Owens!" Charles yelled at the boys. "Run! Run!"

Then he turned Duke's lifeless body face down with his head turned to the side and started pushing his back. After several blows, the boy began to cough out the water and breathe. Thirty minutes later, Duke was able to sit up and talk again. Then Miss Owens arrived.

"What has happened? Is he okay?" she asked. "He's okay," Charles answered. Then he told her the whole story.

Miss Owens looked very upset by the time he was finished. She said, "Alright, you boys, help

Duke walk back to the school. Then we will discuss your punishment."

She turned around and started back to the schoolhouse. The boys followed her in silence, except for Duke. He coughed and choked up water the whole way. When they reached the school, Miss Owens said, "Duke, you stay outside here for a minute. The rest of you may go in and sit with your heads down and wait."

After the others had gone inside, Miss Owens turned to Duke and said, "Well, I am very sorry, young man. I had hoped that you would straighten up after I warned you. Now, however, I have no other choice but to expel you. You may take your things and go home."

That was the last time Charles saw Duke. Soon after that he ran away from home, because he didn't want to live by his father's rules either. Charles was not surprised, however. He was reminded of a verse from the Bible that his mother had read to him many times. "A wise son heareth his father's instruction: but a scorner heareth not rebuke." Mrs. Raymond also read Proverbs 10:1 to Charles. It says, "A wise son maketh a glad father: but a foolish son is the heaviness of his mother."

When Miss Owens went back into the schoolhouse, she was thinking of one certain Scripture. "The rod and reproof give wisdom: but a child left to himself bringeth his mother to shame." Miss Owens knew that she could not let the boys get away easy this time.

Contrary to Charles' earlier dream, none of the other school children envied him. He was spending a lot of time with the other four older boys now. However, they weren't playing. For a whole month, the disobedient children spent their recesses and lunch hours working for Miss Owens.

Chapter 5

CHARLES AND HIS PARTRIDGE TRAP

Mrs. Raymond truly loved Charles. She watched over him faithfully day and night throughout his childhood. One area in which Mrs. Raymond especially tried to teach Charles was the observance of the Sabbath day. Mr. Raymond didn't keep the Sabbath, but his wife did. She taught Charles to observe it also.

Church services were held in the school-house. The town couldn't afford to build both a school and a church, so they used one building for both. When Charles was eight, the farmers had an especially good year. With the extra money they collected for their crops, they bought a new bell for the church. This bell was only rung once a week. That was on Sunday, a half hour before church services.

Every Sunday, Charles and his mother made the journey into town to hear the preacher. They weren't the only ones to travel such a distance for church. Many families came from much farther. Each Sabbath morning, the sidewalks were filled with people on their way to observe the Sabbath.

Those who lived too far away to walk hitched up their wagons and came into town.

Services always started at ten o'clock in the morning. First, the minister took time to explain the Psalm that the congregation would sing. After the song, the families would sit down and hear the sermon. The sermon lasted about one and a half hours. Then they sang another song and closed with prayer.

After the first service, the families sat outside in the schoolyard and ate their lunch. These were always cold lunches that had been packed the night before. The mothers didn't break the Sabbath by preparing food.

At one o'clock, the congregation filed back into the church for the second service. This was in the same order as the first, and they finished at about three o'clock. After the final prayer, everyone went back out into the schoolyard to greet their friends and thank the preacher. Then they left for home.

Most of the families got home by sunset, where they sat down to a cold dinner. After supper, the children repeated the text the preacher used in his sermon, and they discussed what they had learned. Then they went through their Sunday school verses before retiring to bed. All through Charles' childhood, this is how he and Mrs. Raymond kept the whole day holy unto the Lord.

When Charles was eleven, he noticed that not all the boys in the community went to church. Many

Sundays, Charles passed the boys he had gotten into trouble with at the swimming hole. They weren't on their way to church, however. They were usually going fishing or partridge trapping.

Charles began to believe that he was too old to follow the instructions of his mother. His heart turned rebellious, and he felt tied down by her restrictions. Charles wanted to go play with the other boys on Sunday. He wanted to take part in their fun.

Charles knew from experience that it would not be easy to escape his mother's watchful eye. Charles didn't know a truer verse than Ecclesiastes 10:20, "for a bird of the air shall carry the voice, and that which hath wings shall tell the matter." Mrs. Raymond always seemed to know everything that Charles did, good or bad. Sometimes, he wondered if the birds really did tell her.

One Saturday night, however, Charles decided to try to evade his mother just once. All day the snow had been falling. Charles went into town in the afternoon to run an errand for his mother. That evening, on his way home, the snow was about six inches deep. As Charles trudged along the path home, he met Randy. Randy's farm was right next to the Raymonds', so the two boys walked home together.

"Tomorrow would be a fine day to trap partridges," Randy said to Charles. Randy's father didn't keep the Sabbath, and he didn't expect Randy to either.

"Yes, it would," agreed Charles. He was wishing that he could go too. Charles knew that his mother would never let him.

"The thicket in our back field will be full of them tomorrow," continued Randy. "Would you like to go trapping with me?"

Charles slowly answered, "I would like to, but ..."

"Great!" Randy interrupted. "Meet me down at the old well right after you finish breakfast. We'll have a great time."

"Randy," Charles began, "I would really like to go, but I can't. Mother will make me go to church. There is no way that she would let me off to go trapping."

"Oh, Charles, come on. Is that all that is bothering you?" asked Randy. "I know how you can fool her. Just tell her you are sick and that you can't go to church. Don't eat at breakfast. After she is gone, slip into the cupboards and fill your pockets. Then meet me at the well."

The boys had walked as far as they could together. They said goodbye and went their own ways. Charles ran the rest of the way to the house so he could make a trap to use in the morning.

By the time Charles finished the trap it was near dark. Mrs. Raymond came outside to tell him that dinner was ready. She noticed the trap. "Well, what are you making so late in the evening?" she asked.

Charles answered, "Randy said they have a field filled with partridges. I'm going to go catch you some."

His mother said, "Well, you can't go now. Dinner is on the table. You know that tomorrow is the Lord's day. We will be going to church. Now put that silly thing away until later and go get ready for dinner."

"Mother," he said, "I'm not making it for tomorrow, I'm making it for Monday. I'm going to go trapping Monday." To avoid danger, Charles had told the first lie.

Charles felt uncomfortable all night. When he went to bed, he couldn't sleep. The lie he had told filled his mind. He tried to pray but couldn't. Charles couldn't rest until he promised God and his own conscience that he would never lie again.

Charles awoke early the next morning. He lay in bed and thought about his feelings the past night. After a few minutes, he got up and said his prayers. He got dressed and went outside.

A fresh layer of snow had fallen during the night. The sun was beating off the white surface. "It really would be a perfect day for partridge trapping," thought Charles. Then the cry of the partridges overcame all his resolutions from the night before.

Charles remembered that he had promised Randy to meet at the well. Charles knew that he would either have to lie to his mother or lie to Randy. "A lie is a lie," Charles thought, "I might as well tell the one that will be more fun." Charles began forming a plan to deceive his mother. No doubt, Satan helped him.

At breakfast, Charles began showing the signs of his sickness. He pretended that he couldn't eat and groaned a great deal. While everybody else ate, Charles drank a small cup of tea and tried to look pale.

At the end of the meal, Charles looked weakly at his mother. He asked, "Mother, I don't think I can make the walk to church today. May I stay home? I am feeling so very sick."

"Yes, you may stay," she answered, with a question in her eyes. "However, you will have to memorize the one hundred and sixteenth Psalm. You may recite it to me when I get home."

Mrs. Raymond got her things together and left for church.

As soon as she walked out the door, Charles ran to his bedroom to get his cap and gloves. Then he looked out the window to make sure she was out of sight. He couldn't see her, so he flew out the door and to the barn. Charles got his trap and headed for the well.

Randy wasn't the only person that Charles found at the well. Mrs. Raymond was waiting for him also. She had guessed what he was doing and went there instead of to church.

"What do you have to say for yourself, Charles?" she asked.

Randy wasn't the only person that
Charles found at the well.

"I'm sorry, Mother," he answered, miserably. The whole situation suddenly overwhelmed him. Charles understood what he had done.

"Are you sorry for being caught, or are you sorry for lying to your mother and breaking the Sabbath?" she asked.

Charles fell silent.

"Give me your trap," she commanded. Charles handed it to her, and she threw it down into the well. "Let's go home."

When they got back to the house, Mrs. Raymond said, "Sit down in the chair, Charles. I want to talk to you."

She went and got her Bible and handed it to him. "Read Isaiah 58:13-14 to me," she directed.

Charles read, "If thou turn away thy foot from the Sabbath, from doing thy pleasure on my holy day; and call the Sabbath a delight, the holy of the Lord, honourable; and shalt honour him, not doing thine own ways, nor finding thine own pleasure, nor speaking thine own words: Then shalt thou delight thyself in the Lord; and I will cause thee to ride upon the high places of the earth, and feed thee with the heritage of Jacob thy father: for the mouth of the Lord hath spoken it."

"You caused God great displeasure by breaking His Sabbath today, Charles. That was not the only commandment you broke. Besides breaking the fourth by not keeping the Sabbath, you broke the ninth by telling a lie. You also broke the fifth by disobeying me."

She continued, "Ephesians 6:1-2 says, 'Children, obey your parents in the Lord: for this is right. Honour thy father and mother; which is the first commandment with promise.' You have been a very bad boy today, and the Lord tells me that I must discipline you for that. He says in Proverbs 13:24, 'He that spareth his rod hateth his son: but he that loveth him chasteneth him betimes.' Hebrews 12:11 says, 'Now no chastening for the present seemeth to be joyous, but grievous: nevertheless afterward it yieldeth the peaceable fruit of righteousness unto them which are exercised thereby.'"

Mrs. Raymond loved Charles very much. Therefore, after she had prayed with Charles, asking God to bless obedience to His word, she did not spare the rod. Charles' heart was touched.

He said, "I am so sorry for lying to you. I won't tell another lie again, and I will always keep the Sabbath. It was just so easy to keep telling lies after I told the first one. I am so glad that you caught me today, or I might have never stopped telling them. It could have been my ruin. Please forgive me, Mother. I truly am sorry."

"I forgive you, Son. You must ask God for forgiveness too," she instructed.

Charles went back into the house and got washed up for church. They hurried into town and just made it in time for the second service.

Charles spent the walk home thinking about what his mother had told him earlier that day.

"Mother," he asked, "what does it mean to honor your parents?"

"Well, Charles, it means that you must obey our commands cheerfully. When we ask you to do something, you must do it right away. You cannot pretend that you are not able to or say that you don't want to. Always obey your father's and my commands as quickly as possible."

She continued, "Honoring your parents comes from the heart. You don't do it out of fear of punishment. Jesus said in Matthew 5:16, 'Let your light so shine before men, that they may see your good works, and glorify your Father which is in heaven.' When you dishonor your parents, you bring disgrace upon them and upon God."

"Some children dishonor their parents by not submitting to their judgments," Mrs. Raymond told her son. "They forget that their parents have already learned many lessons from experience. There are many different ways that you can honor your parents, Charles. Honoring your parents is very important. It is the only commandment with promise. God says that if you honor your parents, he will make your days long upon the earth."

By this time, they had reached the house. It was about time for dinner. Mrs. Raymond began getting out the cold food to put on the table.

Charles stood in the kitchen and thought for a minute. Then he asked, "Mother, may I set the table for you?"

Mrs. Raymond gave her son a knowing smile and answered, "I would be honored."

One of Charles' first jobs was to plant corn. He walked
along the furrows and dropped in the seeds.

Chapter 6

THE SECOND LIE

At twelve years old, Charles left school to start working on the farm. Since he saw no hope for furthering his education, he determined to study on his own. Charles spent his days working in the fields and his nights reading books.

At first, Charles was content with the books his father had. Those quickly ran out, however, so Charles looked elsewhere. He borrowed books from other adults in the community. Over the years, he read a very large assortment.

During the day, Charles worked on their farm. When he first started working, he expected to be in charge of some of the field hands. After all, he was the boss' son. That didn't seem to matter to Mr. Raymond. He started Charles out at the lowest job, just like everybody else.

One of Charles' first jobs was to plant corn. He walked along the furrows and dropped in the seeds. It was very easy work, but it made his back-ache. He had to carry a heavy sack of seeds up and down the rows for hours. The sun beating down from overhead made it especially uncomfortable.

On the way home from the field after his second day of planting, Charles stopped at the old well for a drink. Randy, his next-door neighbor, happened to stop at the same time.

"Corn planting sure can make you thirsty," Randy remarked.

"It sure can," Charles answered, as he gulped the cool water from the bucket.

"I was thinking about going fishing tomorrow. Do you want to come?" Randy asked.

"I can't, Randy. I've got to plant. We still have two more fields to finish. It will probably take all day. Sure would be fun, though."

"Charles, sometimes I wonder about you. Getting out of planting right now is as easy as can be. The measles are going around. All you have to do is pretend you have the measles. Everyone will be so upset that they will insist you stay home all day."

"Do you really think it would work?" Charles asked.

"Of course it will. It's really easy. Right before you go to breakfast, rub your face real hard. Do it until you turn red and your face feels hot. Then pinch with your fingernails all over your face and neck. That looks like little measles are just about to appear. If you look like that, your mother will never let you work."

"Okay, I'll try it," Charles answered. "Then I'll meet you at the fishing hole as soon as I can."

That night while he was in bed, Charles remembered the partridge trap. He thought of all the good instruction he had received. This only created a feeling of guilt for the sin he was about to commit. Charles still hadn't been totally cured of lying. He still wanted to gratify his evil desires more than he wanted to follow God.

Charles reasoned to himself, "I can't really compare this to the partridge trap anyway. I'm not breaking the Sabbath. Plus, I already promised Randy that I would go. I would be lying to him if I didn't." Having successfully talked himself into the lie, Charles rubbed his face and pinched it all over.

"Mother," he said in front of all the other workers sitting at the breakfast table. "I'm feeling sick. I think I might have the measles. I talked to Randy on the way home yesterday. He said that he had them. I tried to not get too close to him, but it didn't work. I think I have caught them."

The first thing Mrs. Raymond did was have Charles take his shirt off. She knew that one of the first symptoms of the measles was a rash on the chest. She found his skin to be perfectly white. Within a few minutes the marks wore off his face also. Charles' lie was exposed.

"Son," said Mrs. Raymond, "you have lied to me in front of all the other workers. It is only just that you are punished in front of them also. Proverbs 22:15 says, 'Foolishness is bound in the heart of a child; but the rod of correction shall drive it far from him.' You have left me no other choice but to discipline you."

Mrs. Raymond took Charles into the kitchen and applied the rod of correction. While the rest of the workers finished their breakfast, Mrs. Raymond took Charles into this room to talk.

"Charles," she said, "no sin grows more rapidly than lying. If you succeeded in telling a lie today, you will find it much easier to tell a lie tomorrow. The habit of telling them will become so strong that you will hardly be able to speak the truth. If you have already formed the habit, beg the Lord for grace never to tell another. At once, you must break off this habit that leads to disgrace. It makes you a companion of the devil. Jesus said that the devil was a liar from the beginning."

She continued, "You can also tell a lie by holding back part of the truth. Ananias and Sapphira, his wife, did this. They were smitten by God and died instantly, as a warning to all liars.

"Charles, did you realize that liars are despised more than any other sinner? A thief takes your property, but a liar robs you of your character. They disturb the entire community. Lying will disgrace your father and I. It will ruin your soul if you persist. You will learn to hate yourself. You will carry a worm in your bosom that will never die. You will always dread detection and fear exposure. You must always tell the truth, at all costs."

Then Mrs. Raymond reminded her son of the story about George Washington. His father bought him a new hatchet. The next morning he cut down a beautiful cherry tree, which his father loved. No one saw him do it, and he could have easily blamed one of the servants. George didn't, however. He told his father that he could not tell a lie. His father embraced him with a joyful heart and cheerfully forgave him because he told the truth.

"You can learn a lot from that story, Charles," Mrs. Raymond said. "Let your motto be, 'truth under all circumstances.' People of truth are respected. Liars gradually become ashamed to look anyone in the face. No liar has a frank, open countenance. They always look down. If you live by the truth, you will be able to hold your head up and look people in the face. Though you may have many failings, you will be respected."

Among all the sins Charles ever committed, none ever caused him as much distress. Those who had seen him tell the lie and receive his punishment never let him forget it. They reminded him of his deed almost every day. This led Charles to resolve never to tell another lie. It brought into his soul the first real convictions for sin he ever felt.

He could only look on at a distance.

Chapter 7

MR. RAYMOND DIES

Mr. Raymond was a very wicked man. In his everyday language, he constantly cursed and swore. He talked like this his whole life, and he never went to church. When Charles was young, his father liked to tease him. His favorite joke was to tell his son that he was going to raise him to be a preacher.

At the age of thirteen, Charles had been working with his father on their farm for a year. Mr. Raymond had a custom of rising early in the morning and eating as soon as he was dressed.

One morning, Mr. Raymond rose very early and called to Charles to bring him something to eat. Charles brought a tray of bread, meat, and milk to his father. As Charles entered the room, he could hear his father swearing about the day's work ahead.

When Mr. Raymond saw his food had come, he sat down to eat. He had barely taken one bite when he grabbed his chest. Without another twitch, Mr. Raymond fell to the bed – and in a moment, he was dead! He died of a heart attack.

Charles was the only one in the room. This was the first time he had ever seen someone die. It alarmed him terribly to see this wicked, profane man cut down in a moment. Minutes before, Mr.

Raymond had asked damnation. Charles knew that God had taken him at his word.

"Mother," Charles cried. "Come here quickly."

In a moment, his mother was at the side of her dead husband. She closed his eyes. Charles helped her put him on the bed. Then they called for the neighbors.

His father's unexpected death blasted Charles' hopes for inheriting the farm. Mr. Raymond hadn't taken the time to write a new will after they adopted Charles. Before he had ever hoped of having a child, Mr. Raymond had willed his estate to his brother's son.

Charles now saw no hope in rising in the world, except by his own industry. He still lived with his mother on the farm. However, he didn't have the satisfaction of knowing that someday it would be his.

"Oh, Mother," Charles complained. "What is the use of working so hard day in and day out? Nothing will ever come of it now that I don't own the farm."

"Charles, God's Providences are very mysterious," his mother explained. "Often we receive the greatest blessings from our greatest disappointments. Many people cannot bear riches. You may be one. He may withhold riches from you to save your soul. The Lord may deprive you of them in love and mercy."

"But, Mother, how will I ever succeed if I don't have any money?" Charles asked.

"My dear boy, many of the greatest men in our land started their lives poor. In many ways, the poor child has an advantage. He must depend on his own energy and God's blessing to build his fortune and character. When a wealthy child with no character loses his property, he has nothing left. I have found that those who earned their own way in life eventually fill high positions. Take heart in these examples, Charles."

A few months later, Charles met another trial. Charles' natural mother lived in a town about seven miles from Bradburry. Throughout his childhood, Charles kept in limited contact with her. He did not know her well. He had seen her enough, however, to know that she was a very godly woman.

Just a few months after Charles' father died, an epidemic of smallpox broke out in their area. The boy's natural mother was one of the first victims of the illness. The panic was so great over her death that Charles wasn't even allowed to attend the funeral. He could only look on at a distance.

The deaths of these two people in Charles' life served to be a great lesson to him. The one had died a sinner, with no hope or repentance. The other, a servant of God, died in peace. She had lived her life with a heart that was truly in God's fear. Through this, Charles saw the reality of Malachi 3:17-18, "in that day when I make up my jewels; and I will spare them, as a man spareth his own son that serveth him. Then shall ye return, and discern between the righteous and the wicked, between him that serveth God and him that serveth him not."

The death of Mr. Raymond played a great part in the developing of Charles' character. It drew him from trusting in man to relying more on God. The death of his natural mother served a great example to Charles. He knew that she died in peace, because she had lived a life in the service of the Lord.

These two events put a conviction into Charles. In the year following his mother's death, he strove to learn all he could. During this period, Charles read all the books he could. At nights, Charles sat by the fire, reading most of the books in the neighborhood.

Charles also grew an overwhelming desire to become a preacher. Many times he tried to find out if he was a true Christian or not. He would go into the woods and ask God to speak to him. Charles asked God to tell him if he was saved or lost.

Sometimes, Charles quit praying altogether. If he was lost, Charles reasoned that his prayers would only increase his misery. Other times he prayed on and on, in hopes he would lessen his suffering if he did go to hell.

While the other boys played, Charles studied. On the Sabbath, he always attended church services. Still his despair remained. Charles felt God's afflicting hand upon him. In order to appease God's anger, Charles read and prayed more. With all that, he still remained an enemy of God. He served the Lord through slavish fear, not through love.

Finally, Charles asked his mother for guidance. Mrs. Raymond explained to him how God chastens those he loves. She read to him Hebrews 12:5-7, "... My son, despise not thou the chastening of the Lord, nor faint when thou art rebuked of him: For whom the Lord loveth he chasteneth, and scourgeth every son whom he receiveth. If ye endure chastening, God dealeth with you as with sons; for what son is he whom the father chasteneth not?"

Mrs. Raymond said, "Charles, the poor publican offered one of the best prayers. 'God be merciful to me a sinner.' He felt what he said, and God answered him in mercy. The first work of the Holy Spirit is to convict the world of sin, and of righteousness, and of judgment."

"Charles," the wise lady continued, "until the Spirit convicts you of your sin, you won't pray right. You mustn't make this an excuse to quit praying, however. Praying will make you quit sinning, or sinning will make you quit praying."

She went on, "A child living without prayer is like a boat in the midst of the mighty ocean. The boat is without a pilot or a rudder. It tosses about on the furious waves. Soon it will sink, and it will never rise again. Don't let this happen to you, dear Charles."

They led him into his next step, which was gambling.

Chapter 8

CHARLES BECOMES PROFANE

During the first few months after the death of his natural mother, Charles studied all he could. Instead of playing with the other boys, he stayed home and read books. This not only increased his knowledge, this also inflated his pride.

Charles frequently overheard adults saying that he was the smartest boy in the neighborhood. The constant shower of compliments puffed up his spiritual pride. Charles began to feel very important. When Charles' Uncle Jake took over the farm, several changes were made. The biggest change concerned the hired help. Uncle Jake replaced all of the older farm hands with young men who were a few years older than Charles. Charles didn't mind this, because now he had other young men on the farm near his own age.

These young men brought with then some very bad habits. They swore and chewed tobacco. They stayed up late into the night playing cards and were almost never on time for work.

Charles watched the way these men acted. Feeling very important, Charles decided that he must start being a man. He foolishly thought that if he could swear and chew tobacco, too, he would be a full-grown man. Charles started imitating these profane men.

At first, Charles found swearing to be rather awkward. The other field hands laughed and laughed at his attempts to curse. Charles didn't give up, however. Eventually, he picked up this vulgar, God-insulting vice.

After he started swearing, Charles became afraid of being alone, especially at night. He was scared of lying down in a dark room. He feared that God would cut him off and send him to hell. During these times, Charles prayed and promised God that he would stop swearing.

The next day, when he went back out in the fields with the other young men, Charles forgot his promises. He would even venture a little farther each time. Little by little, he began ignoring his conscience.

After Charles mastered swearing, he started chewing tobacco. The field hands gave him the tobacco and showed him how to chew it. The first time Charles tried the tobacco, he thought he was supposed to swallow it when he was done. The field hands were quite amused by Charles' reaction.

For Charles, swearing and chewing tobacco were not enough. They led him into his next step, which was gambling. The other young men stayed up until late in the night playing cards and gambling. Many times after dinner, Charles would sneak out of his bedroom window and go watch.

Charles did quite well in picking up these bad habits. There was one area where Charles fell behind. That was in the want of money. Charles only had one French crown from selling partridges. That was worth one dollar and ten cents.

Through the want of money, God saved Charles. The madness of gambling had complete control over him. Often, he sat up all night and played until all his tobacco was gone. If Charles had had any money or could have obtained it, he would have spent it too.

Among all the corruptions to which human nature is addicted, perhaps gambling brings the greatest ruin. It has a tremendous power of fascination. Special grace is required to escape its grasp. Gambling brings with itself a long line of sin. It can lead to theft, lying, drunkenness, and much more.

Charles kept his swearing, chewing, and gambling a solemn secret. He tried to keep it from his mother and the other religious people of the community. Somehow, however, Mrs. Raymond found out.

Mrs. Raymond started watching her son very closely. She doubled the number of Psalms he had to learn to prevent him from having time to spare for gambling. She hoped to fill his mind with God's truth. She believed it would ultimately cast the devil out of Charles' heart, through the operating of the Spirit.

Mrs. Raymond also sat Charles down and talked with him about it. She said, "Charles, flee from the deadly powers of these sins. If you don't, they will produce a moral paralysis that will deaden your soul to every virtuous emotion. These sins will harden your heart to every crime.

"The God who made you commanded, 'Enter not into the path of the wicked, and go not in the way of evil men,' Proverbs 14:4. He also said in 1 Timothy 5:22, 'Abstain from all appearance of evil.' Charles, you must be cautious. You might blot out your every hope for heaven."

For some months, this process went on. For Charles, the inward struggle was severe. The force of truth, coming in contact with the inclinations of an unrenewed heart, often made him feel life had become a burden. This struggle destroyed every enjoyment of his sin.

Up until this time, Charles attended church regularly. The more he sinned, the less he went to church. He didn't feel justified to walk into the church when he had spent the night before gambling. The more he swore and took the Lord's name in vain, the harder it became for him to pray.

The other people of the town took notice. They knew Charles had been a boy of strict upbringing. The Christian character of his pious mother suffered from his wickedness.

Charles also suffered. He appeared to be happy, but he was terribly miserable. His conscience stung him like a scorpion, and his agony became almost unbearable.

Much later in his life, Charles learned to mourn over his sin. He began to realize the influence he had made on others. The oaths he swore, many other children learned and repeated. They repeated it to others, and its consequences would run on forever. Charles knew that he had added fuel to a fire that never dies.

Charles took the book home and began reading it that night.

Chapter 9

FALSE RELIGION

The Holy Spirit continued to work on Charles' conscience. He found no rest in sin. God still worked grace in Charles, so the struggle became severe. When Charles was alone, he wept and prayed. He resolved to break away from sinning and turn to God.

When his flesh gained control a few hours later, he wished he had never seen a Bible. He wanted the parts of the Bible that condemned his sins to be left out. Sometimes, he even tried to persuade himself that the Bible wasn't true. Of course, Satan was ready to suggest doubts and rebellion. Charles thought about many things but not about the one thing needful: Jesus Christ.

Until this time in his life, Charles had never met anyone who denied the great evangelical truths of Christianity. Neither had he read any books on religious subjects, other than the Bible.

One day, when Charles was sixteen years old, his Uncle Jake sent him to town to pick up some goods from the store. While Charles was in town, he met an old schoolmate, Ken. He was one of the boys who Charles ran off with to the swimming hole.

Ken had just recently returned from the east coast. After finishing school, he moved out there to look for work. During his stay in the East, Ken got married. His wife came from a family that believed in Universalism.

Universalism is the belief in universal redemption. Universalists believe that every man is saved no matter what he does. The result is the attitude that we can sin all we want, because we will be saved anyway.

Ken was zealous about his new faith. He was anxious to share it with Charles. Ken invited Charles over for dinner, so he could tell him all about it.

Over dinner, Charles listened with deep interest to Ken and his wife. Charles found that his conscience couldn't agree with it, although, he wished that it might be true. This religion would fit him perfectly.

Charles didn't hate sin, but he was very preoccupied with the consequences of sin. Charles only had a legal religion. Charles thought that a religion which would allow him to sin all he pleased without any fear of its consequences, would suit him.

During the dinner, Charles thought of all the Scriptures he knew which should prove the theory wrong. Every time he asked his friend about one, Ken talked his way around it. Charles started to wonder if this religion could possibly be real.

The whole time, Charles felt a strong desire for his friend to remove all doubt from his mind. Charles thought of all the sins he had never tried, because he was too afraid. With this new religion, he could do them all. Charles wanted Ken to convince him that the doctrine was true.

"Charles," Ken finally said, "I have some books on the subject if you want to read them. Here, I will give you this one to start with." Charles eagerly took the book about the atonement of Christ.

Charles took the book home and began reading it that night. Before he finished it, Charles started making plans to fulfill all of his evil desires. His moral restraint nearly disappeared. Charles was trying the sins which had made him shudder only a short week ago.

When Charles finished the first book, Ken gave him another. This one explained the parables of Jesus according to Universalism. Charles read with delight until he came to the parable of the rich man and Lazarus. Charles found the author's reasoning to be foolish and extreme. This blasted his newly found hopes.

Charles went back to Ken and said, "Have you read this book?"

"Yes, wasn't it wonderful?" Ken asked.

"What did you think about the parable of the rich man?" Charles questioned him. Charles wanted Ken to assure him and remove all his doubts.

"Well, Charles, I advise you to do what I have done. That is to accept this doctrine as unquestionable. Then you will soon understand all the parts of it."

By this time, Charles was willing to do anything to sin with an easy conscience. He followed Ken's advice.

Mrs. Raymond found one of these books in Charles' drawer when she was putting the wash away. She sat down and looked through it. The book horrified her. She had never heard of such blasphemy in her life. When Charles came home, she asked to speak with him.

"Son, I remember one of Miss Owens' favorite sayings," she said. "'Show me your company and I will tell you your character.' Charles, this book was written by an evil person. Every moment you spend reading this book, you are spending with that person. You cannot rub your hands in filth without some of it sticking on you."

Mrs. Raymond continued, "Charles, you cannot read these books without harming yourself. You are trying to play with fire without getting burned. It is hard enough to keep your heart under control. You don't need another force pushing you closer and closer to sin. When you take away the doctrine of God's displeasure against sin from the religious creed, you have taken away your last hope for true evangelical repentance."

"Shun these books," his mother warned. "Let the Bible be your daily companion. Read books which tell you to turn from sin. God's word tells us to decide who are sent by Him. Jeremiah 23:21-22 says, 'I have not sent these prophets, yet they ran: I have not spoken to them, yet they prophesied. But if they had stood in my counsel, and had caused my people to hear my words, then they should have turned them from their evil way, and from the evil of their doings.'"

Charles listened to what his mother had to say. For almost a year, he couldn't make up his mind as to which way he would follow. The scales rose and fell in proportion to the power of conviction of sin or the inclination to yield to temptation.

Two great powers were working in his heart. One was striving to lead Charles deeper into sin. The other cried into his ear, "Turn ye, turn ye from your evil ways; for why will ye die?" The struggle was long and fierce. Unfortunately, Charles chose to fall deeper into sin.

Charles spent the next four years of his life proclaiming Universalism. Throughout it all, he still had a small voice warning him, "The soul that sinneth, it shall die." While Charles was with his friends, he could roll sin like a sweet morsel under his tongue. When Charles was alone, hell would flash up before him with all its horrors. Charles felt that the pains from his guilty conscience in one hour overbalanced all the sinful pleasures of a week.

Charles was tangled in the meshes of Universalism, but he had an old barbed arrow of truth in his conscience. Sometimes, this arrow held him back from committing the sins. Other times, his will to sin overcame it.

Of all the false systems of religion, none is better suited than Universalism to gratify the depraved human nature. Denying punishment for sin offers the reins for every lust. It gratifies every unholy desire. In the end, Universalism gives the meanest and vilest humans the reward of sitting on the right hand of God.

Finally, at the age of nineteen, Charles was overcome by the truths his mother taught him. He remembered that when he was a boy, he promised God he would become a preacher. All of his broken vows had a powerful effect. Charles finally realized that Universalism was wrong. He knew that he could no longer ignore the Bible truths he was taught throughout his childhood.

Chapter 10

CHARLES PROPOSES

During Charles' fight with Universalism, he dated many of the girls of Bradburry. Charles grew quite fond of one in particular. Her name was Susan Harrison. They were very close, but Charles wasn't ready to ask her to marry him. First, he wanted to go farther out West.

While he was working in the fields, Charles heard that his neighbor, Randy, was going back to Ohio. In those days, Ohio was known as the far West. Charles asked him if he could go with him. Randy was glad to have the company, so Charles said goodbye to Susan.

In Ohio, Charles and Randy spent their time clearing land and hunting deer and bears with the Indians. Among other days, the Indians hunted on Sunday. They invited Charles and Randy to go with them. Randy accepted at once.

At first, Charles hesitated. The thought of desecrating God's holy day frightened him. Charles remembered what his mother had said about the partridge trap. Charles turned down the invitation in order to keep the Sabbath.

After a few weeks, Charles hunted without any remorse.

At once, Randy started laughing. "Come on Charles. Sunday hasn't even come this far west yet. Real men don't go to church, Charles, they hunt."

Charles couldn't stand Randy's sneers. He got his gun and followed him.

For Charles, it was a horrible day. He spent the whole time worrying that some sudden judgment of God would fall on him. He didn't shoot his gun, because he feared it would backfire and kill him. At the end of the day, Charles was surprised to be alive. He didn't think God would permit him to live for his awful sin.

Since Charles thought he got away with it the first time, the second time was much easier. When he got ready to go the next Sunday, Charles' conscience felt better. After a few weeks, Charles hunted without any remorse.

Randy and Charles stayed out west for six months. During this time, Charles saw a preacher only once. Charles didn't attend one worship service, and he didn't keep one Sabbath. His conscience had almost ceased to warn him.

When Charles went home, the restraints, which he had scarcely felt before, became almost intolerable. The silence of the Sabbath was as distressing as a funeral. Charles longed to be where he wouldn't feel the restraints of religion. Charles wanted to live where all the appetites and passions of his heart could be indulged with public consent.

Charles still labored to throw off the truths of the Bible, embedded in his memory from his childhood. He flattered himself that he would gain enough sinful pleasure on earth to make up for the loss of heaven. Charles' rebellious heart refused to yield to the voice of God, yet He continued to work with mercy and love in Charles.

Upon returning to Bradburry, Charles felt lost. Charles desperately wanted to escape the farm. Charles knew that he must provide for his wants. At the same time, he wanted to find the best chance for sinful gratification. Charles wasn't accomplishing this under the watchful eye of his mother.

He reasoned that the best way to do this would be to start a new career. Only, Charles wasn't sure what he wanted to do, so be started asking different people around Bradburry what they thought. Some said, "Join the military, Son. That is a career for a real man." Others advised Charles to travel back East in search of work.

For Charles, the suggestion of a stranger, who happened to pass through Bradburry, was the best. The stranger told Charles that the East coast was teeming with ships looking for crews. He said that if Charles was looking for a real adventure, all he needed to do was get a stagecoach ticket to the coast. Charles could get on the crew of one of the ships and sail all around the world.

At last, with hopes of escaping from his mother's lectures and all other religious restraints, Charles resolved to go to sea. Without telling anyone, Charles met the next stagecoach with his bag in hand.

Just as Charles was going to pay for the ticket, he started having second thoughts. Storms and shipwrecks rose to his view. Filled with doubt, Charles decided to wait. These thoughts were too intolerable for him to bear.

Finally, Charles determined to ask God which course he should pursue. Charles knew that he was an enemy of God, but he saw no other option. In this state of mind, Charles left for the woods alone. He went to lay his case before Him who sees the end from the beginning.

While in the woods, Charles remembered what his loving mother had taught him. God is wroth with sin. Charles knew he was a sinner. Mrs. Raymond taught him a holy reverence for God's revealed will. She always referred to it as the fear of God.

Charles took out the Bible he brought with him and turned to some of the Scriptures Mrs. Raymond had read to him so long ago. He turned to Psalm 112:1 and read, "Praise ye the Lord. Blessed is the man that feareth the Lord, that delighteth greatly in his commandments."

Then he turned to Ecclesiastes 12:1. His mother always told him that the wisest of all men said this in the Spirit of Christ: "Remember now thy Creator in the days of thy youth, while the evil days come not, nor the years draw nigh, when thou shalt say, I have no pleasure in them."

Charles recalled the time his mother taught him not to tell lies. She read to him Revelation 21:8, "all liars, shall have their part in the lake which burneth with fire and brimstone."

Then Charles remembered one of his friends that had died very young. Charles tried to imagine where the boy's soul had gone. He would have given half a kingdom to know all that soul knew in a few hours.

These thoughts led Charles to pray and promise God he would cease from sin. He vowed to give God his strengths and talents. All these emotions were the work of God's Spirit. God was using His own truth and providence toward others as a means of leading Charles to repentance and delivering him from the power of sin.

Charles remembered something that Mrs. Raymond once told him, but that he never really understood. She said, "If some kind friend woke you in the night, warning you that you must leave immediately because your house was in flames, wouldn't you escape that moment? Would you ever forget that friend? Wouldn't the sound of their voice send a thrill of joy through your heart ever after?" Now, Charles understood that Mrs. Raymond had been talking about God saving him from sin.

Now, Charles began to realize what Jesus said in Luke 6:46-49. "And why call ye me, Lord, Lord, and do not the things which I say? Whosoever cometh to me, and heareth my sayings, and doeth them, I will show you to whom he is like: He is like a man which built a house, and digged deep, and laid the foundation on a rock: and when the flood arose, the stream beat vehemently upon that house, and could not shake it: for it was founded upon a rock. But he that heareth, <u>and doeth not</u>, is like a man that without a foundation built a house upon the earth; against which the stream did beat vehemently, and immediately it fell; and the ruin of that house was great."

Then he began to understand Revelation 3:20. "Behold, I stand at the door, and knock: if any man hear my voice, and open the door, I will come in to him, and will sup with him, and he with me."

God brought Charles to realize that he would be held responsible for his actions. He had spent a good part of his life running away, denying, hiding from, or flat-out disobeying the truth. Now, it was time for him to repent and turn from his sin.

Charles resolved that his first change would be to start taking responsibility. Going to the coast would be running away, so Charles discarded that notion. He thought, "What else can I do though? I am getting too old to burden Mother by taking care of me. She will never let me leave without a good reason."

Then the most logical answer rushed to his head. "Susan. I can ask Susan to marry me. She would make a wonderful wife, and I finally feel responsible enough to take care of her."

Within a few months of his afternoon in the forest, Susan gave Charles her consent to marriage. Neither Charles nor Susan were rich, so they realized that they would both have to work. Charles would find a labor job, and Susan could take in sewing at the house. Both had been brought up to work hard, so this was quite feasible.

Charles took on his new duty sensibly. He abandoned all his former evil habits and limited himself to honest labor. Doubtless, this marriage saved Charles from becoming a wanderer. Charles often wondered about the mysterious Providence of God. Charles frequently recalled the verse in the Bible which says that a good wife is from the Lord. Now, Charles began to understand how true it was.

Chapter 11

STRUGGLING FOR FAMILY WORSHIP

After their marriage, Charles and Susan lived in the town of Bradburry for one year. Charles worked at a lumberyard, hauling lumber. Susan took in sewing. They saved every spare cent they had. Finally, they saved enough money to rent a small piece of land. Charles started farming to support himself and his wife. They bought one workhorse and one old plow. Charles built a small shack from lumber and tar paper to live in.

Charles spent many hours in deep, anxious thought. He worried about how he and his wife would survive. His days of pleasure were at an end. Now, he faced the realities of life. Charles labored and toiled from sunrise to sunset. Daily, he repeated to himself, "There is no peace for the wicked."

Susan worked equally as hard. They did well for being so poor, but their future looked dark and dreary.

Charles often fretted about his lot. At times, he even wished that he had never been born. With these feelings, he had an abiding conviction for sin. Indeed, that was the main cause of his anxiety.

71

Six months after Charles and Susan moved onto the farm, Charles became very ill. He had inflammatory rheumatism, which caused excruciating pain. The doctor traveled five miles from town every day for three weeks to see him. After the doctor had done all he could for Charles, he told him that he was going to die.

The young man twisted with agony of soul at the thought of being dragged into the presence of God with all his sins unpardoned. Charles felt that he deserved the deepest hell. He had shut his heart against the calls of God's Word and Spirit thousands of times.

The Bible, the sermons, his pastor's counsel, and his mother's warnings stood against him as the witnesses for God. They all testified as in Proverbs 1:24, "Because I have called, and ye refused; I have stretched out my hand, and no man regarded."

God seemed to be laughing at his calamity and mocking at his fears. For many days, Charles felt suspended over hell without hope of escape. He was a helpless, unpardoned sinner in the hands of an angry God. The angel of death and his own conscience pursued him, saying Amen to the justice of his damnation.

All the pleasures of Charles' past sins could not make up for one hour of his present agony. His past sinful enjoyments had now become his eternal tormentors. He strove to banish them from his sight as they rose up before him in their hideous deformity. The more he struggled, however, the closer they clung to him. They drove their fangs all the deeper.

He strove to give his heart to God in the midst of these sufferings. He promised, if God would spare his life and restore him to health, he would dedicate the remainder of his days to His service. In this state of mind, Charles tried to pray. There seemed to be no God to hear, however, and no Savior to intercede. He felt no Spirit to comfort his wretched soul.

In a few days, Charles started to feel better. He even began hoping for a recovery. Charles' prayers were answered. To the astonishment of all who saw him, in a few weeks, Charles could walk about and attend to a little business.

Because of his long sickness, he lost most of his crop. The doctor's bill amounted to near all he was worth. Fall was approaching, and Charles could not raise another crop until spring. To provide for his wife through the winter and pay the doctor's bill, Charles got a job in the general store in town. He and Susan rented a room above the store for the winter.

As Charles began to gain strength, he felt a strong desire to return to his former habits and to associate with his old companions. Charles had no religious friends his own age. For months after he recovered, Charles was not allowed to go outside, even to church. The doctor feared he might go into a relapse.

Charles had no other religious people near him. His wife was not religious, and the store keeper's family wasn't either. His Bible was his only means of religious instruction. Charles was surrounded by people who denied God. Still, Charles vowed to keep the promises his soul had made in anguish.

One day a few months after Charles started working, a friend from his early childhood came into the store. Charles immediately recognized Bill. They used to sit together after church while their mothers talked.

Charles and Bill talked for a while. They recounted the time since they had last seen each other. It had been many years.

Bill asked, "Do you still attend church?"

"Not since my illness. I cannot go outside until springtime, when it is warm. I sure wish I could, though," Charles answered.

Bill said, "My pastor gave me an excellent book to read. It's called 'The Afflicted Man's Companion.' Would you like to borrow it?"

Charles got the book and read it with deep interest. It reminded him of all the promises he made when he was sick. When Charles was through reading the touching book, he resolved to live and die the death of the righteous, with God's help.

Charles now began struggling in earnest. He found he had a carnal heart. Satan's influence supported it and resisted God's Spirit. It held up Christ as too merciful to punish a sinner eternally.

Charles reasoned, however, that the punishment of his sickness was inconsistent with the characteristics of a merciful God. If eternal punishment was unjust, punishment on earth must be unjust also.

The agony of his soul was so great that he often went up into the attic of the store and struggled with his thoughts for hours. He had no religious friend to whom he could reveal the feelings of his heart. His wife and all around him, as far as he knew, lacked any feeling on the subject of religion. If they had known his feelings, they would have ridiculed him.

Charles strove to surrender himself to Christ, but in vain. A voice seemed to follow him continually. The voice repeated Mark 8:38 to him, "Whosoever therefore shall be ashamed of me and of my words in this adulterous and sinful generation; of him also shall the Son of man be ashamed, when he cometh in the glory of his Father with the holy angels."

After a long struggle, Charles felt that his only relief would be public acknowledgment of Christ and His cause. Still, he shrunk from the duty. Charles wanted to be a secret Christian. He wanted to go to the Savior, like Nicodemus, in the night season.

Charles stayed in distress for several months without relief. He finally determined to ask a blessing at his table. His wife had just given birth to their first child. Charles wanted his son to grow up in a godly home. This seemed to be a hard task before an irreligious wife. He took the challenge and succeeded.

The news soon spread. The neighbors asked Charles and his wife to dinner so he could give the blessing at their tables, but he refused. This reminded Charles of the fearful text, Mark 8:38. For some time Charles declined dinner invitations if he expected to be called on to ask a blessing at the table.

Once Charles got this far, he felt he must go a step further. He decided to begin family prayer. Susan had recently discovered that their second child was coming, and Charles wanted to welcome it into a godly environment. Charles knew that they needed to pray as a family.

Every Sunday night for six months, Charles tried to start the prayer. When the time came to call his wife and son to pray, Charles' courage failed. Charles spent hours in the attic praying to God for strength. However, when night came and the moment drew near, he would tremble with fear and retire without prayer.

Charles' conscience lashed out at him for being ashamed of Christ. This state of mind continued until life became a burden. He wanted to abandon his own soul from his mind and lead a moral life. Charles thought that if he did go to hell, it couldn't be much worse than his present misery.

The Spirit of God still strove in his heart, however, and would not give up. Charles finally resolved to begin family worship or die in the attempt. The baby was coming soon, and he must start. He set the next Sunday night to begin. He felt stronger on Sunday than on any other day. Also, there was less danger of anyone coming in at night than in the morning.

Charles spent most of that Sunday in prayer. Then the dreaded hour arrived. Satan and an unrenewed heart resisted the Spirit of God. Duty and shame, together with the offspring of sin, made Charles tremble. Susan was entirely ignorant of the struggle in his heart. As Charles began to speak, his voice faltered.

Susan asked, "Is there something wrong, dear?"

Charles could not reply. The struggle was awful. He was at the point of resolving never to try a family prayer. Then a voice seemed to say, "Go forward now, or you will seal your doom."

Charles saw this as a turning point in his eternal destiny. He felt that heaven or hell hung on that moment. Two unseen powers seemed to have the death-grip. The moment of final decision was there. After a few minutes of silence, Charles arose and grasped the Bible with a trembling hand. He was determined to read a chapter and pray or die in the attempt.

He broke the silence by saying, "My dear wife, God has said He will pour out His fury on the families that call not on His name. I am compelled to begin tonight. Will you join me?"

She said nothing.

*Charles opened the Bible. The struggle was
over, and his fears left.*

Charles opened the Bible. The struggle was
over, and his fears left. Man's extremity was God's
opportunity. He felt the precious promise in 2
Corinthians 12:9, "And he said unto me, My grace
is sufficient for thee: for my strength is made perfect
in weakness. Most gladly therefore will I rather
glory in my infirmities, that the power of Christ may
rest upon me." Charles performed the duty, and the
peace of God filled his heart.

Susan looked alarmed, but she remained silent. Charles told her of his long struggle. She seemed deeply impressed for a long time but did not give evidence of a change of heart for many years after.

From that day on, Charles felt the power of what the apostle Paul said in Romans 7:22-25, "For I delight in the law of God after the inward man: But I see another law in my members, warring against the law of my mind, and bringing me into captivity to the law of sin which is in my members. O wretched man that I am! Who shall deliver me from the body of this death? I thank God through Jesus Christ our Lord. So then with the mind I myself serve the law of God: but with the flesh the law of sin."

Chapter 12

PASTOR JOHNSON'S VISIT

After Charles took the steps of bringing prayer into their family, he felt a strong desire to bring in more religious teaching. He still wasn't allowed outside, so he couldn't go to church. The only other way for Charles to see the minister was to invite him in. The next time Pastor Johnson came into the store, Charles invited him over for dinner.

After the Pastor arrived that evening, he and Charles sat down to talk while Susan finished making dinner. Charles told him of the struggles in his life. The Pastor listened intently.

When Charles was through, Pastor Johnson told him about grieving the Spirit of God. He said, "The Spirit of God is the agent between God and dying men. When the Holy Spirit withdraws, you cannot find any comfort in the atonement and intercession of the Son of God."

Then the preacher read to Charles certain Scriptures from his Bible concerning this subject. He read Genesis 6:3, "And the Lord said, My spirit shall not always strive with man, for that he also is flesh: yet his days shall be an hundred and twenty years." From there the Pastor turned to Ephesians 4:30 and read, "And grieve not the holy Spirit of

God, whereby ye are sealed unto the day of redemption." Then Pastor Johnson read 1 Timothy 5:19. "Quench not the Spirit."

"Charles," the Pastor directed, "The Holy Spirit is the third person of the adorable Trinity. He is sent by the Father and the Son to apply the atonement of Christ to the heart of the sinner. We can find the first work of the Spirit in John 16:8, 'And when he is come, he will reprove the world of sin, and of righteousness, and of judgment.'"

Charles listened with deep interest to the pious man's instruction.

He continued, "When He reproves, or convicts the heart of sin, He awakes in the sinner's heart and mind serious thoughts of eternity. He does this by pressing on the heart some of the warning truths of the Bible. The sinner may have heard these truths very often before without being affected. Now, they make him tremble. Business or pleasure may drive these feelings away, for a time, but they will return again and again."

Charles understood the truth of the preacher's words. That very thing had happened to him. Charles remembered how he had become occupied with Universalism for many years, but the truth still returned to him.

Again, Pastor Johnson referred to his Bible. This time he read Ephesians 2:1. "And you hath he quickened, who were dead in trespasses and sins." The Pastor explained that when the Spirit quickens a soul from spiritual death, He continues to strive against the desires of the flesh. Then he explained that this is the Spiritual warfare spoken of in Galatians 5:17, "For the flesh lusteth against the Spirit, and the Spirit against the flesh: and these are contrary the one to the other: so that ye cannot do the things that ye would."

At this time, Susan interrupted them to say that dinner was ready. Charles and Pastor Johnson went to the table, but they continued their discussion over dinner. Susan looked rather stunned, but she listened quietly.

Pastor Johnson explained how those whom the Spirit has quickened feel sin to be such a grievous burden that they must forsake it. They must cast themselves on Christ with their whole heart. Then the Holy Ghost, by His almighty power, renews their heart and enables the sinner to surrender himself to the will of God.

Pastor Johnson explained to Charles that when this happens, the sinner is born again. He becomes a new creature in Christ Jesus. His distress of mind vanishes. It is replaced with joy and peace. As an evidence of the change, the very things he loved most before, he now hates. The things he once hated, he now loves. He desires Christians for his companions. He loves the ministers of Christ. He loves the house of God. He loves to read the Bible and pray. He shuns the company of the wicked in whose society he once delighted. His constant aim is to become more holy and more like Christ.

The Pastor's words seemed to be recounting Charles' past perfectly. They made Charles realize how sinful it is to grieve the Holy Spirit. As the Pastor continued, Charles remembered his past.

The wise preacher said, "Let me tell you the various stages of feeling through which you will pass before becoming converted or being given over to hardness of heart and blindness of mind. We may see how near to the line of everlasting separation between God and your soul you may have come.

"The Spirit of God most often begins to move on the hearts of those who have been brought up in the '... nurture and admonition of the Lord.' The process begins when you are still very young. Your example, Charles, is not rare. Many feel these convictions of the Spirit while they are still very young."

Charles recalled these convictions and strivings of the Spirit and all the time his mother had spent trying to teach him the ways of the Lord.

The Pastor continued, "I have reason to believe that many are truly quickened by the Spirit in their early periods of life. Between the ages of fifteen and twenty, multitudes have felt His saving influence. Most of those who ever give evidence of being born again, experience the quickening of the Spirit before the age of twenty. This is what happened in your case, Charles."

Then the Pastor asked, "Hasn't a feeling of awful solemnity sometimes passed over your soul, which made you think of God's displeasure upon

Charles nodded in agreement.

sin? Have you ever thought about how you could spend eternity with a Holy God whom you have never learned to love?"

Charles nodded in agreement.

Pastor Johnson continued on. He read from Revelation 21:23, "And the city had no need of the sun, neither of the moon, to shine in it: for the glory of God did lighten it, and the Lamb is the light thereof."

"Charles," he implored, "Jesus said in John 3:19, 'And this is the condemnation, that light is come into the world, and men loved darkness rather than light, because their deeds were evil.' How do you think you can ever enter that heavenly city where Christ's righteousness shines brighter than the sun, with secret sins hidden in your heart?"

Charles said, "My mother has taught me that only those who desire to come to the light will ever enter heaven. When I was young, she explained to me what Jesus said in John 3:21, 'But he that doeth truth cometh to the light, that his deeds may be made manifest, that they are wrought in God.'"

Pastor Johnson said, "The fruit of the quickening of the Spirit is a change of heart. A truly converted heart desires to come to the light that they may see their sins and turn from them."

Then the preacher asked, "Have your sins ever risen up before you and broken your rebellion against God? Has this ever made you desire to be a Christian? Have you never promised God that you would turn to Him and lead a life in His service?"

"Yes, many times," Charles answered.

The preacher related, "you probably couldn't tell where this feeling came from. It might have been from hearing a sermon or receiving a kind warning from some friend. It might have happened while you were reading a religious book. These feelings have returned again and again."

Charles recalled aloud, "I remember the time when these same kind of feelings returned to my heart. My convictions of sin became deeper. I formed new resolutions to serve the Lord and seek a pardon for my sins. Then nothing came of it. Within a few days, I was back to my old ways."

"Yes," agreed the preacher, "I understand what happened. It has happened to many. Through your good intentions, Satan got you to think you could stand in your own strength. That is why your resolutions lasted for only a short while."

Pastor Johnson instructed, "When the Spirit begins His work, He continues to strive with you. Have you spent anxious days and nights during revivals of religion? Some special truth may have fastened on your mind, yet it gave you no peace. You saw others embracing the Savior and rejoicing in hope, which only increased your distress. A voice seemed to call to you, 'My son, give me thine heart, and let thine eyes observe my ways.'"

Charles said, "Yes, that is what happened. Then I began to count the cost. I knew that if I became a Christian, all my youthful pleasures would end. To get rid of these feelings, I stayed away from the house of God. I went to places of worldly entertainment. I associated with thoughtless sinners. By this, I hoped to banish all the convictions of sin. Now, I know that this is what Scripture calls, 'Grieving the Spirit of God.'"

By this time, they had finished their dinner. Charles and the preacher talked more while Susan cleared the table.

Charles continued recounting his past. He explained, "After awhile, a revival season returned. The arrows of conviction flew thick around me. My sins rose in awful majesty before me. I felt as if hell was yawning beneath me. The Spirit of God said to me, 'Now is the accepted time.' Heaven seemed open before me. The Savior was ready to embrace me. Then the spiritual warfare became more and more intense. Another voice from within me cried, 'There is time enough yet! Religion will destroy all your pleasures; live on for a few years as you are.'"

The Pastor warned of the great danger of grieving the Spirit. He pointed out, "Thousands now in hell have reasoned in the same way as you just experienced. No doubt, they meant to attend to the subject, as you do now. Every day, however, they delayed the work of repentance, and the wall of separation between God and them rose higher and higher. So it will be with you, if you continue to grieve the Spirit of God until old age. By such a course, your heart continually grows harder. The same truths that made you tremble five years ago are, perhaps, scarcely felt now. Thus the hardening process goes on, until the day of grace is past."

Then the Pastor said, "O awakened sinner, while the Spirit strives it is the day of grace. Do not sit down to count the loss of sinful pleasures. Count the cost if you should lose your soul! Pray for grace to forsake your sin and plead for a pardon for your soul. Pray that the Holy Spirit will reveal the Savior in your heart, and you will have pleasures lasting for eternity."

Charles felt greatly encouraged.

The Pastor continued, "Pleasures in Christ leave no sting behind. They will sustain the soul when on your dying pillow. They will remain when the last trumpet shall sound and the congregated world stands before God.

"Many flatter themselves by thinking that as they grow in grace and knowledge, they will enter on this and other duties. The only way to grow in grace is performing our duties in the Spirit of Christ, in reliance on God. You might as well expect to increase your bodily strength without taking food, as to increase spiritual strength without secret and family prayer."

Then the Pastor said, "I must go now, but let me leave you with some advice. As the blacksmith's arm gains strength by swinging the hammer, so will you gain strength in the performance of spiritual duty. God bless you, son."

⚬✖⚬

*He followed a narrow footpath along the
side of a high hill that led to his house.*

Chapter 13

CHARLES GOES
TO CHURCH

Throughout the rest of the winter, Charles continued with the family worship. When spring came, he took Susan and the two children with him to the farm. After the family had made the move out of town, Charles got in touch with the Pastor of the church. He wanted to start bringing his family to church.

The Pastor told Charles to give the church a full statement of his past experiences on the next Sunday. When the day came, Charles laid before the church his spiritual struggles and his present spiritual condition. Then he waited outside of the schoolhouse while they decided if he could be admitted into the full fellowship of the church.

The elders unanimously agreed to grant Charles the full privileges of the church. He trembled at the news, because he did not feel fit to go to the Lord's table. Pastor Johnson urged all his members to examine themselves through prayer before coming to the communion table on the next Sabbath.

Charles spent that week in deep anxiety and almost unceasing prayer. He longed to know, if possible, how matters stood between God and his own soul.

Charles expected to have some unmistakable evidence of God's presence while at the Lord's table. He formed this idea from what he had heard ministers say to other communicants. He had often heard the Pastor refer to the Lord's table as a testing place, where Christ met His people to bless then. The Pastor had said that they could ask large things of Him while they were there, expecting He would grant them.

Charles partook of the Lord's supper the first time under this impression. He was looking for some sensible manifestation of God's presence. Unfortunately, to his utter astonishment, he experienced nothing of the kind. He left deeply distressed and disappointed.

Charles returned home under the impression that he had eaten and drunk damnation to his own soul. He thought he had committed the sin spoken of in Matthew 12:31, "Wherefore I say unto you, All manner of sin and blasphemy shall be forgiven unto men: but the blasphemy against the Holy Ghost shall not be forgiven unto men." Charles' distress was now greater, if possible, than before. He spent the night in deep anguish of soul, and the morning brought no relief.

The next day Charles returned to the church to attend the application service, as was usual in that part of the country. He was so distressed that he couldn't pay attention to the sermon. Charles spent the whole time anguishing over the sin he thought he had committed against the Holy Ghost.

Charles walked home by himself that day, because a neighbor offered to give Susan and the children a ride. There wasn't enough room in the wagon for Charles too.

On the way home, his soul was burdened with the deepest distress. Life seemed to be intolerable. He desired to die and know the worst of his case. Charles felt tempted to destroy himself.

He followed a narrow footpath along the side of a high hill that led to his house. Hunters were the only ones who commonly used the trail. The trail passed along a dark cave. Charles left the path and went into it. No eye but that of God could see him there. Charles resolved to remain until he found peace with Christ.

Charles cast himself on the ground in the cave. Agonizing, he cried, "Lord, save, or I perish." Instantly, an indescribable joy full of glory satisfied his soul. Heaven seemed to come down to earth with all its enrapturing delights. Charles felt like the disciples on the mount of Transfiguration. He arose from the earth feeling as if he could almost fly heavenward.

The happiness, which followed, was better than all the pleasures of his whole past life put together. Charles had received a foretaste of the good Word of God and the world to come. Everything looked beautiful; all nature appeared changed. When he reached home, it seemed different from before. God seemed to be in him and everything around him.

This state of mind continued unabated for some weeks. Charles spoke and thought only of Christ and his salvation. He performed the toils and labors of the day without the usual fatigue or weariness.

> *Not a wave of trouble rolled*
> *Across his peaceful breast.*

Alas, the lurking pride of Charles' heart began to show itself. He began to feel as if he had become a favorite in heaven. As his self-righteousness increased, his heavenly-mindedness decreased and doubts arose. He wondered if all the joys he had experienced were an illusion. He thought Satan might have transformed himself into an angel of light and thus deceived him. Charles began to feel deep anxiety.

The spirit of prayer had left Charles in a great measure, and heaven seemed closed against his cries. However, he was still unwilling to give up religious duties. Charles determined that if he did perish, he would perish at the foot of the cross, so he would continue to pray.

After a few weeks, light dawned again on his soul. Charles had hope that he was a child of God. In future years, he believed that his heart had changed the night he first worshiped God in the presence of his wife, more than six months previous.

He had long prayed for clear evidence that he was a child of God. He prayed that his happiness might be complete, and he might be free from the fear of death. God gave Charles the desire of his heart for a short time, in order to show him his own weakness. The Lord used these trials to teach Charles that his strength was not in himself, but in God, and thus to teach him a lesson of humility.

Spending a day in heaven and feasting upon its pleasures would not serve as an unmistakable evidence of his acceptance with God. Even such evidence, unsupported by daily grace, could not deliver Charles from falling into doubt, darkness, and perplexity. The Lord gave him grace enough to prevent despair, and not enough to lead to presumption.

*Several boys and girls, mostly children of
godless parents, were learning to read the Bible.*

Chapter 14

CHARLES AND THE SUNDAY SCHOOL

The cares of this world began to press hard upon Charles. He was very poor and had nothing but his own hands to depend on for a living. Many a day he rose while the stars were still shining and went out into the fields. After working all day, he returned again by starlight with little to show for his labor.

Charles truly earned his bread by the sweat of his brow. His lot seemed a hard one. When he was a little boy, he often prayed Agur's prayer, "Give me neither poverty nor riches; feed me with food convenient for me." Even from looking at that prayer, he could hardly understand his plight.

Charles wanted to embark on some new endeavor, but the dread of failure prevented him from doing so. He feared that others might lose something through him. Charles feared that he might stain his character and religion.

By constant toil, in a few years the production on his plot of land began to improve a little. During wet days and the long nights, he read religious books, storing his mind with spiritual knowledge. These religious books became his daily companions.

Charles knew they would better develop and improve his heart and mind than any other reading.

Soon after uniting with the church, he felt that he must do more for Christ's cause on earth. Drunkenness, Sabbath-breaking, and many other sins surrounded him. Charles started wondering what he could do to remove them.

About that time a very pious man, a few years older than Charles, bought a plot of land a few miles away. This Mr. Prescott organized a Sunday school in his home. As soon as Charles heard of the school, he went to see it. It was the first one established in that area.

This Sunday school attracted quite an amount of attention. The old-fashioned Christians thought it was a violation of the Sabbath. They denounced it in bitter terms. Other Christians had heard of these schools from their relatives in the East. They were thoroughly excited about the new addition to the community. Charles decided to see for himself and judge accordingly.

Charles visited the school on the next Sunday after church. He watched very closely. Several boys and girls, mostly children of godless parents, were learning to read the Bible. From seeing these children, who certainly could have died without ever seeing a Bible, Charles felt it was a good work.

At the close of the study, Mr. Prescott asked Charles to lead in prayer. He declined, because he had never prayed in the presence of anyone except his wife. After all the children were gone, Mr.

Prescott took some time to talk with Charles about the school.

"Mr. Prescott, I think this is a wonderful work you are doing. These children are given the chance to read the Bible. That surely wouldn't have happened if it weren't for you," Charles admired.

"Thank you for your praise," he answered, "but I am afraid I won't be able to continue at this pace by myself. The school is becoming rather large. If it grows much more, I won't be able to handle the duty."

"What will you do then?" Charles asked.

"Well, I will have to find someone to help me," Mr. Prescott answered. "Do you know of anyone who might be interested?"

Charles pondered the idea for a moment, and he knew that this was his duty. This man's piety was so far above any he had ever met that it impressed him deeply. He seemed to breathe the atmosphere of heaven. Charles answered, "I will help you, Mr. Prescott. I would be delighted to be doing such a godly work."

Before they parted, Mr. Prescott gave Charles a book to read for the next Sunday school class. Charles also agreed to come back that evening after supper for a prayer meeting. Trembling with fear and embarrassment, Charles offered to take part in the exercises.

This began a new era in Charles' life. While he felt humbled with his own defective performances, he felt an approving conscience in striving to do his duty. He had new views and new feelings. His soul fired with new zeal. He determined to enter the field and labor for souls as one that must give account to God.

The next week Charles came to the Sunday school after church and helped Mr. Prescott. He invited all his neighbor's children to attend. Mr. Prescott's house quickly filled, and a neighbor who had a larger house kindly offered it for use. He accepted the offer, and that house soon filled.

The community built a large building for the school and for other means of education and moral improvement. A few months after the new school house was built, Mr. Prescott had to move on. He left Charles in charge of the Sunday school. Charles now felt that he was doing some good to others, as well as making progress in his own spiritual life.

In addition to his Sunday school, Charles opened his house for a weekly prayer meeting. Charles conducted this alone. At these meetings, he usually read from a book of sermons.

A year after this school and prayer meeting began, a deep religious interest manifested through all the community. Through his connections with Mr. Prescott, Charles arranged for traveling ministers to preach in private houses. In a few months, more than fifty people gave evidence that they had been "born again". Many of these people had attended the Sunday school or prayer meetings.

This was the first revival of religion Charles had ever seen. His Christian character became strengthened by it. He increased in both power and knowledge to do good. As a result of the revival, Charles was ordained one the elders of the church.

This brought a very unexpected problem. Charles dreaded the responsibility of the office, because his wife felt violently opposed to it. She was upset about the loss of his time and extra expenses. She had never shown any disposition to encourage him in religious duties but rather threw obstacles in his way.

For peace at home, therefore, Charles declined the duty of being an elder for a short time. His Christian friends begged him to tell why, but love forbade his giving them the reason. Conscience urged Charles to do his duty, and he finally determined to forsake all and follow Christ. He would strive to win her over to Him and His cause.

After seeing what a good teacher Charles was, the community asked him to help out in the regular school. Charles took on the responsibility eagerly, and he began teaching many students. He knew several of the young children from his Sunday school.

This new responsibility required all his energies. During the recesses he made his lesson plans for the Sunday school, and he memorized the Scriptural texts of the lessons. Charles was kept busy day and night.

This constant labor of body and mind pushed Charles into a relapse of his previous illness. Again the doctor thought that Charles was going to die.

During this sickness, many a touching scene occurred at his bedside. Some of his pupils were with him every day. They shed tears of sorrow as they received his dying counsels. None came or went unwarned.

On one occasion, a married woman who had learned to read in Charles' Sunday school came to see him. As she stood by his bed, Charles asked her where her soul would be if she were in his position. She wept and trembled, and returned home a mourning penitent. She soon found peace in believing. She lived the rest of her life as a repentant Christian and died rejoicing in hope of glory.

At another time, Charles' family and many of his neighbors had gathered around his bed to see him die. At this time, God took pleasure to manifest Himself in a special way. Heaven, with all its glories, seemed to unveil itself to Charles. He longed to depart and be with Christ. At his bed stood a weeping wife with two poor and helpless little children.

Beside his wife stood some of his students and many others in their sins. Before Charles, heaven seemed to be open with all its glories to receive him. His physical frame was nearly a skeleton. The ordinary foregoings of death were nearly all past.

The tears of his wife and little children stirred all the feelings of his nature. The suspense of his mind was awful; the struggle severe. At last he cried, from the innermost recesses of his heart, "O,

Lord, if it be for thy glory, and the good of never dying souls, let me live; if not, let me die." God's will was that he should live.

Charles learned that all who enter the service of their divine Master have trials to meet. The Christian's life is a constant warfare. The great archenemy would follow him at every step and would often bring trials when they are least expected. Satan often presented the discharge of religious duties as a great burden. Thus he tried to frighten Charles back to his service; and if he yielded once, the difficulty increased.

When Charles made a determined effort to rely on God, the difficulty would vanish. God would meet him and help him through. When the Israelites became entrapped at the Red Sea and at the command of God went forward, the sea dried up before them.

Charles neglected his duty to God and his own soul for his wife. When he changed his mind and decided to obey God, opportunity opened up to be a witness to his wife for Christ. Charles knew that he must forsake father, mother, sister, brother, wife or husband when they came between him and Christ. Charles read in 1 Corinthians 7:16, "For what knowest thou, O wife, whether thou shalt save thy husband? or how knowest thou, O man, whether thou shalt save thy wife?"

Charles knew that God has promised that he who watereth shall be watered. All faithful laborers for Christ meet a gracious reward even in this life.

Every soul who "shall believe on Christ through their word," will be a star in their Redeemer's crown.

Chapter 15

SUSAN BECOMES A BELIEVER

Upon being raised up from the verge of death, Charles gave unceasing attention to his Sunday school. His scholars increased rapidly in Bible knowledge. At every communion, a few would make a public confession of their faith in the Redeemer. Some fathers and mothers sat with their children as pupils to study God's Word and embraced Christ with them.

In addition to his Sunday school, Charles kept holding the prayer meetings two or three times each week. He experienced some of the sweetest moments of his life during these social gatherings. God seemed to come down into their midst. The very atmosphere imparted a divine stimulus to their souls. In a few months, many precious souls were won over to the Lord's side and publicly professed faith in Christ.

These constant meetings increased Charles' domestic troubles. His wife viewed them only as time lost. Susan called his new joy "wild enthusiasm." This pained his heart and often drove him to tell his sorrows to God. Charles spent many evenings in a lonely grove on the bank of the creek running through their land. The murmurs of the stream mingled with his agonizing groans for the salvation of Susan's soul. No one but He who rules the heavens knew of this.

At last, the time came when his sorrow would turn to joy. God answered Charles' feeble prayers. The ministering angels rejoiced at the end of one communion Sunday. That day Charles earnestly renewed his request, at the communion table, to the great King for the salvation of his wife.

Until returning home, Charles didn't discover anything unusual. When he went to put away his horse, Susan followed him. With tears, she said, "My dear husband, I am a great sinner." Susan sank down onto the ground and asked Charles to pray with her to God to have mercy on her. Charles and his wife prayed together to their Savior to save her soul.

On that day, Susan changed her conduct for the rest of her life. She encouraged her husband in all his labors; their home was blessed. She was as the help meet spoken of in Genesis 2:18. Every good work filled her heart with heavenly peace.

Charles soon felt it was his duty to visit the sick, to talk and pray with them, and bury the dead. This gave him many opportunities for doing good. Since reading religious books had helped to lead him to Christ, Charles purchased all of these that he could and lent them to his neighbors. The books opened the way for religious conversation. As a result, he reached many that neglected all other means.

In due time, Charles resolved to visit all the families in his neighborhood. He entered the first house trembling in fear. With much stuttering, Charles told them the reason of his visit. As soon as he made it known, the burden fell from his back. His stammering tongue loosened. Charles experienced as God said to Paul, "My grace is sufficient for thee; my strength is made perfect in weakness." All his fears disappeared. The visit was a successful one, and God watered Charles in return.

He spent all that day going from house to house. He talked and prayed with his neighbors, distributed tracts and loaned books. Two Scriptures rang in his ears: Proverbs 29:25, "The fear of man bringeth a snare: but whoso putteth his trust in the Lord shall be safe." And Mark 8:38, "Whosoever therefore shall be ashamed of me and of my words in this adulterous and sinful generation; of him also shall the Son of man be ashamed, when he cometh in the glory of his Father with the holy angels." These urged Charles on, and at last, he resolved to attempt it in the strength of God.

Charles continued from day to day, until he visited all the neighborhood. Christians became roused to duty, and some sinners became awakened to see their need of a Savior. They showed an interest in his prayers and asked for renewed visits.

One incident encouraged Charles so much that he resolved to devote all his leisure time to this work. During a visit, he turned to an extravagant young man and asked if he kept the Sabbath.

"No," the young man answered, in a sneering manner.

"Have you ever been concerned about the fate of your soul?" Charles asked.

He replied, "Not really."

Charles then implored the man, in the most urgent manner, to attend at once to the interest of his eternal soul. Charles concluded by saying, "You might be in eternity before the light of another day. You may be on a sick-bed, from which you will never rise."

The young man was touched and began crying. That evening he went to bed in usual health. At midnight, he awoke very sick, and the earlier warning of the evening rushed to his mind. In a day or two, he sent for Charles, who found him very sick and deeply distressed about his soul. He was very ignorant of the plan of salvation. His parents were not religious, and he had never been taught it.

The fever soon fell into his lungs, and all hope of his recovery disappeared. Charles visited the man's bedside several times before he died. During most of the time, the man's agony of soul was great; but God, for Christ's sake, spoke peace to him.

Immediately, he began pleading to all who came to see him to flee from the wrath of God, especially his parents. He entreated them with tears to forsake their sins and turn to God. Charles added his own prayers. Both of the man's parents promised to reform and seek their soul's salvation. They wanted to meet their son in heaven. When the man died, his soul was filled with peace and overwhelmed with joy.

Charles aided in conducting the funeral services and gave his parting counsels to the family. This case encouraged him to greater urgency for the souls of others. It removed his timidity in talking to all whom he met. Charles resolved never to spend another hour with any person alone, without speaking to them of the ways of God and the value of their soul.

Many years later, when Charles was traveling to the East, he met a nice young man. As was his custom, Charles addressed this man very seriously on the subject of salvation. While he was explaining to him the doctrine of the new birth, the young man interrupted. He said, "It seems as if you have studied your Bible thoroughly."

The reply seemed significant to Charles. He asked, "Are you a Pastor, sir?"

The stranger replied, "Yes, I am."

Charles told the man of his promise made some years ago. Then he said, "I hope I have not offended you. I am truly sorry."

"An apology is not necessary," the young pastor replied. "You have given me a reproof I shall never forget. I am making the same promise right now. I will not spend another hour alone with someone, without speaking to him of his soul and eternity. In heaven, undying souls may be stars in Christ's crown, resulting from this very promise."